POKÉMON

COME MEET MARILL AND MORE

BY SIMCHA WHITEHILL

Ready to discover the world of Pokémon?
Inside this book you'll meet some of the
cutest, most popular Pokémon in the
Johto region. Just turn the page to start
your Pokémon quest.

ISBN 978-0-545-21476-6

© 2010 Pokémon. © 1995-2010 Nintendo/Creatures Inc./GAME FREAK inc.™
and ® and character names are trademarks of Nintendo.
All rights reserved. Published by Scholastic Inc.
SCHOLASTIC and associated logos are trademarks and/or registered trademarks of Scholastic Inc.

12 11 10 9 8 7 6 5 4 3 2 1   10 11 12 13 14 15/0

Cover Design: Henry Ng   Interior Design: Kay Petronio
Printed in the U.S.A. 40
First printing. August 2010

SCHOLASTIC INC.

New York   Toronto   London   Auckland
Sydney   Mexico City   New Delhi   Hong Kong

MEET THE POKÉMON TRAINERS

Ash Ketchum is a Trainer who wants to become a Pokémon Master! His best buddy, Pikachu, is always by his side.

ASH

Brock is a breeder who knows a lot about Rock-type Pokémon. He and Ash have been pals for a long time.

BROCK

Dawn is a Coordinator who is traveling on her Pokémon journey. She has become a good friend to Ash and Brock.

DAWN

Jessie, **James**, and **Meowth** are Pokémon thieves! They steal Pokémon from other Trainers. Luckily, they aren't very good at it.

TEAM ROCKET

BELLOSSOM

FLOWER POKÉMON

FUN FACT Bellossom love to dance to the beat of their own petals, which rub together and ring like bells.

CELEBI
TIME TRAVEL POKÉMON

STATS

According to legend, Celebi watches over the woodlands as a guardian.

How to say it:
SEL-ih-bee

Type: Psychic-Grass

Height: 2' 00"

Weight: 11.0 lbs.

FUN FACT

Celebi has the power to travel anywhere in time, but it only chooses peaceful places to visit.

CORSOLA

CORAL POKÉMON

Corsola must live in clean seas, so many choose the crystal-clear waters of the south.

How to say it:
COR-so-la

Type: Water-Rock

Height: 2'00"

Weight: 11.0 lbs.

Some amazing towns are built on top of a layer of Corsola.

DELIBIRD
DELIVERY POKÉMON

Delibird like to build their nests along tall cliffs.

How to say it:
DELL-ee-bird

Type: Ice-Flying

Height: 2' 11"

Weight: 35.3 lbs.

6

A Delibird does errands for Team Rocket. Jessie, James, and Meowth asked it to deliver a Yanma to their boss.

ELEKID

ELECTRIC POKÉMON

FUN FACT Once electricity is built up, Elekid can blast it out of its body like lightning.

FURRET
LONG BODY POKÉMON

FUN FACT Furret's tail is so long, it's impossible to tell where its body ends and its tail begins!

HOUNDOUR
DARK POKÉMON

STATS

When Houndour are hunting, they signal each other with special barks.

How to say it:
HOWN-dowr

Type: Dark-Fire

Height: 2' 00"

Weight: 23.8 lbs.

FUN FACT Houndour always roam around in packs. If they get separated, they can listen to howls to find the pack.

9

LARVITAR
ROCK SKIN POKÉMON

Larvitar can munch on mud pies. They are born underground and have to chow down to find their way out of the dirt.

How to say it:
LAR-vuh-tar

Type: Rock-Ground

Height: 2' 00"

Weight: 158.7 lbs.

 FUN FACT

After Larvitar eats an entire mountain, it falls into a deep sleep so it can grow.

LUGIA

DIVING POKÉMON

STATS

Lugia is a Legendary Pokémon who guards the ocean. It rests deep down at water's bottom.

How to say it:
LOO-gee-uh

Type: Psychic-Flying

Height: 17' 01"

Weight: 476.2 lbs.

FUN FACT

Some believe that if Lugia flaps its wings, it can cause a storm that lasts forty days.

11

MAGBY

LIVE COAL POKÉMON

12

Even Magby's snot is hot! With each breath, Magby drips burning embers from its nose and mouth.

# MANTINE
KITE POKÉMON

Mantine can swim so fast they fly out of the water!

How to say it:
MAN-tine

Type: Water-Flying

Height: 6' 11"

Weight: 485.0 lbs.

FUN FACT

Mantine travel together in schools, but they're also found with hungry Remoraid, who hang on for the ride.

MARILL

AQUA MOUSE POKÉMON

STATS

The ball on the end of Marill's tail helps keep it afloat. It's filled with special oil that's lighter than water.

How to say it:
MARE-rull

Type: Water

Height: 1' 04"

Weight: 18.7 lbs.

14

FUN FACT Ash, Brock, and Dawn met a new friend, Lyra, when they found her lost Marill.

PHANPY
LONG NOSE POKÉMON

STATS

Phanpy might be small, but it's so strong, it can carry a grown person.

How to say it: *FAN-pee*

Type: Ground

Height: 1' 08"

Weight: 73.9 lbs.

Ash once traveled through Johto and won a Phanpy Egg as a prize.

POLITOED
FROG POKÉMON

Politoed can boss others around. They can order Poliwag to do as they say.

How to say it:
POL-ee-toad

Type: Water

Height: 3' 07"

Weight: 74.7 lbs.

16

When three or more Politoed get together, they form a band and sing together in a deep croak.

REMORAID
JET POKÉMON

Remoraid ride on Mantine so they can nibble on Mantine's leftovers.

How to say it:
REM-oh-raid

Type: Water

Height: 2' 00"

Weight: 26.5 lbs.

Remoraid can hit flying prey from an amazing three hundred feet away!

SLOWKING
ROYAL POKÉMON

STATS

The crown on Slowking's head is actually a Shellder whose poisonous bite gives Slowking extra brainpower.

How to say it:
SLOW-king

Type: Water-Psychic

Height: 6'07"

Weight: 175.3 lbs.

FUN FACT

No matter what's going on, Slowking stays cool and thinks things through.

SLUGMA

LAVA POKÉMON

STATS

Slugma are made of lava, just like the volcanoes they live on.

How to say it:
SLUG-ma

Type: Fire

Height: 2' 04"

Weight: 77.2 lbs.

FUN FACT If Slugma stops looking for hot spots, it will cool down and turn hard. So Slugma never stop moving, not even for a second.

19

SMEARGLE

PAINTER POKÉMON

Smeargle uses over five thousand special patterns to mark its territory.

How to say it:
SMEAR-gull

Type: Normal

Height: 3' 11"

Weight: 127.9 lbs.

20

FUN FACT — Smeargle never needs to go shopping for art supplies. Its tail is a built-in paint-and-brush set!

SMOOCHUM

KISS POKÉMON

STATS

Smoochum's lips are very sensitive. It plants its mouth on things to figure out if it will like them.

How to say it:
SMOO-chum

Type: Ice-Psychic

Height: 1' 04"

Weight: 13.2 lbs.

FUN FACT How can you tell Smoochum's about to pucker up? It's hard. Smoochum is often nodding its head as if it's ready to smooch something!

21

SNUBBULL

FAIRY POKÉMON

FUN FACT It's not unusual to find Snubbull cozying up to women. Many women can't resist its scary cuteness!

TEDDIURSA

LITTLE BEAR POKÉMON

Teddiursa makes its own sweet treat by soaking its paws in honey, then licking them.

How to say it:
TED-dy-UR-sa

Type: Normal

Height: 2' 00"

Weight: 19.4 lbs.

Teddiursa has many secret hiding places to store food for the long, cold winter.

23

WOBBUFFET
PATIENT POKÉMON

STATS

Wobbuffet likes to hide out in dark places. Some believe this is because it is hiding its unusual tail.

How to say it:
WAH-buf-fett

Type: Psychic

Height: 4' 03"

Weight: 62.8 lbs.

24

FUN FACT

If anyone tries to bully Wobbuffet, it inflates its body to drive them away.